PLEASE DON'T CHANGE MY DIAPER!

Published by Inhabit Media Inc.

www.inhabitmedia.com

Inhabit Media Inc. (Iqaluit) P.O. Box 11125, Iqaluit, Nunavut, X0A 1H0
(Toronto) 191 Eglinton Avenue East, Suite 310, Toronto, Ontario, M4P 1K1

Editors: Neil Christopher and Kelly Ward
Art Director: Danny Christopher

We acknowledge the financial support of the Government of Canada through the Department of Canadian Heritage Canada Book Fund.

This project was made possible in part by the Government of Canada.

Printed in Canada

Library and Archives Canada Cataloguing in Publication

Title: Please don't change my diaper! / by Sarabeth Holden : illustrated by Emma Pedersen.
Other titles: Please do not change my diaper!
Names: Holden, Sarabeth, 1982- author. | Pedersen, Emma, 1988- illustrator.
Identifiers: Canadiana 20200246569 | ISBN 9781772272734 (hardcover)
Classification: LCC PS8615.04325 P54 2020 | DDC jC813/.6-dc23

PLEASE DON'T CHANGE MY DIAPER!

by Sarabeth Holden

illustrated by Emma Pedersen

The sun is shining.
The birds are chirping.
Look at my puppy's tail sway.
I've got my sled, and I am ready to
play in the snow all day!

3

Off to the park!

Let's get this show on the road!

My puppy wants to go, too, I can tell!

But wait. Oh dear. What is that strange smell?

5

6

I think I know . . . but let's just go!
Don't worry about where it's coming from.
Oh no, what's that you say, Mum?

PLEASE DON'T CHANGE MY DIAPER!

8

The world is falling apart!
It's crumbling all around!
My life is over. The sky is falling to the ground!

PLEASE DON'T CHANGE MY DIAPER!

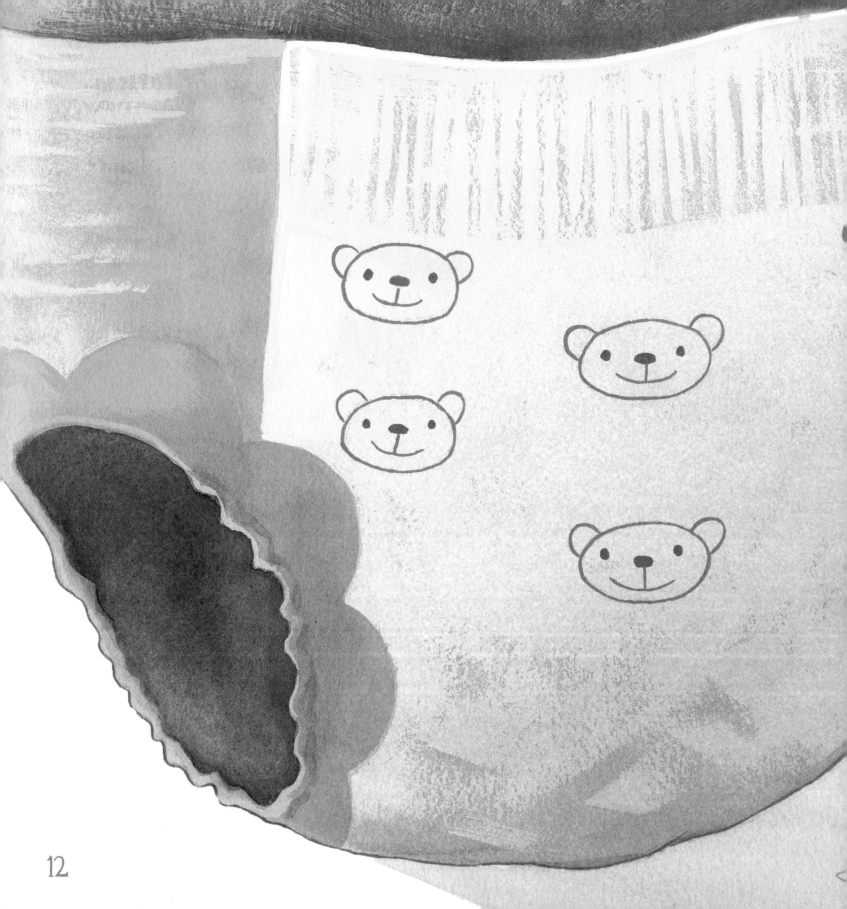

The sun no longer rises!
The moon casts its glow no more!
The end is near. I know it is! The tides no longer
crash against the shore!

PLEASE DON'T CHANGE MY DIAPER!

I will miss my fluffy puppy.
I will miss the sparkly snow.
To my best friends, near and far,
I love you, you must know!

Please don't change my diaper!

Please don't change my diaper!

Please don't change my diaper!

18

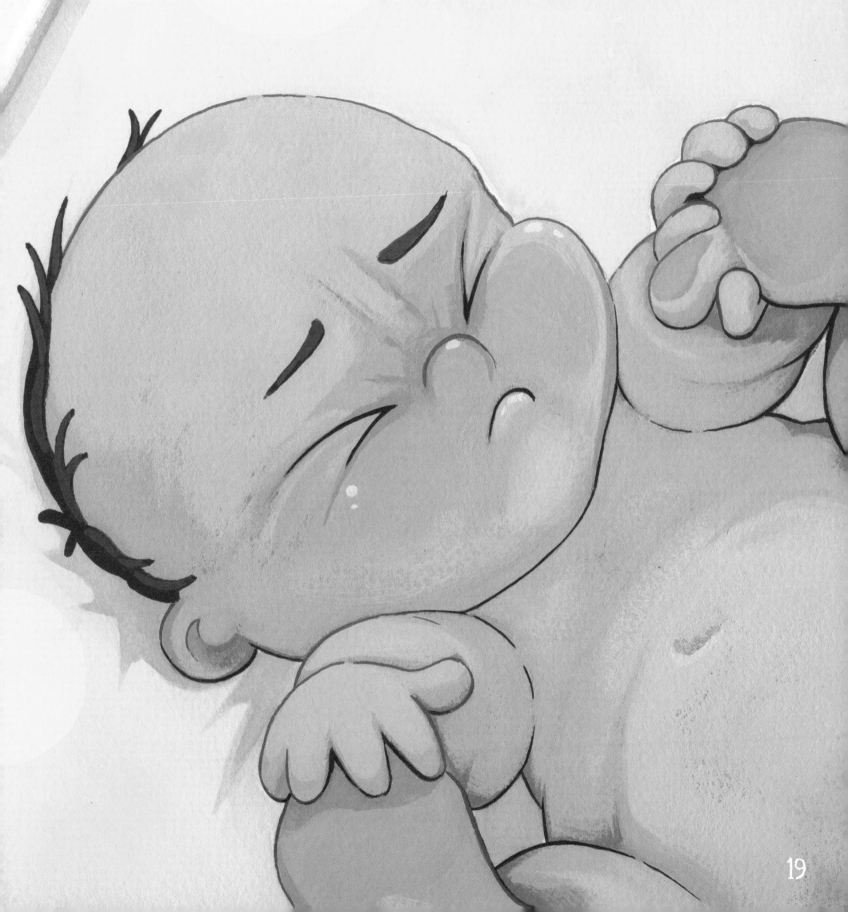

Wait... what is this fresh, delightful feeling?
What's happening now? I don't know.
My mum's arms are wrapped around me as we
rock to and fro.

The world is still turning.
The sun still shines so bright.
My mum, my dad,
my puppy—everyone
is here, to my great delight!

22

I must enjoy this wonderful feeling,
because I know it will soon wane.
In just a few short hours ... maybe minutes ...

the diaper change will loom again!

Sarabeth Holden is an entrepreneur who loves to cook, do yoga, golf, and snowboard. She lives in Toronto with her husband, Sean, their sons, Raymond and Jackson, and their dog, Oslo. The whole crew loves to spend time outside. When they're not outside, Sarabeth enjoys singing made-up songs to make things like diaper changes and face wiping a little more bearable so they can get back to the things they love: blowing raspberries, having kitchen dance parties, and reading stories. Sarabeth grew up in Nova Scotia, Nunavut, New Brunswick, and Ontario, and is now the president of the Toronto Inuit Association, supporting the local Inuit community as it grows.

Emma Pedersen is an illustrator from Toronto, ON. She has a degree in drawing and painting from OCAD University and has also graduated from Sheridan College's illustration program. She mainly works on the publishing side of illustration but has done work in advertising and animation as well. She lives with her husband in an apartment full of books and would love to just be drawing dogs all day if possible.

Inhabit Media Inc.